The Doozer Disaster

By Michaela Muntean
Pictures by Diane Dawson Hearn

Muppet Press
Holt, Rinehart and Winston
NEW YORK

Copyright © 1984 by Henson Associates, Inc.
Fraggle Rock, Fraggles, Muppets, and character names are trademarks of Henson Associates, Inc.
All rights reserved, including the right to reproduce this
book or portions thereof in any form.
Published by Holt, Rinehart and Winston,
383 Madison Avenue, New York, New York 10017.

Library of Congress Cataloging in Publication Data
Muntean, Michaela.
The Doozer disaster.
Summary: Wembley Fraggle, longing for something
exciting to happen to him, picks a giant radish in
the garden of the Gorgs, then falls down the hole
it has left behind.
[1. Puppets—Fiction]   I. Hearn, Diane Dawson, ill.
II. Title.
PZ7.M929Do   1984   [E]   84-6527
ISBN: 0-03-000707-0
First Edition
Printed in the United States of America
1 3 5 7 9 10 8 6 4 2

ISBN 0-03-000707-0

CHAPTER ONE

JUST outside Fraggle Rock there is a garden. In the garden there are turnips and beans and radishes and all kinds of things you would find in most gardens. The gardener, however, is not the kind of gardener you would find in most gardens, because this garden happens to belong to the Gorgs.

Gorgs are very, very big, and not very nice. At least they are not nice to Fraggles. There are many reasons for this, but the most likely reason is that Fraggles, who like to dance and sing and have a good time, also love to eat radishes. And because the only radishes to be found in Fraggle Rock are in the Gorgs' Garden, that's where Fraggles go to get them.

This drives Junior Gorg crazy.

One of Junior's chores is to take care of the Garden. This is a lot of hard work. So you can see why it makes Junior a bit crazy to see his radishes walk off with a pair of Fraggle legs beneath them. Junior sets traps for the Fraggles and would like nothing better than to thump one of them if he got the chance.

Now that you understand the problem, you can see why Mokey and Wembley Fraggle were waiting patiently at the entrance of the Gorgs' Garden until Junior finished raking.

It was Mokey's job to gather radishes, and usually she preferred to gather them alone. She loved the quiet coolness among the leafy green rows of vegetables. It gave her time to think poetic thoughts (besides gathering radishes, Mokey Fraggle writes poems).

This particular day, however, was unusual, and it was unusual for two reasons. First, the radish supply was alarmingly low. Second, on the way to the Gorgs' Garden, Mokey ran into her friend Wembley, who was sitting on a rock twiddling his toes and singing a song.

"Gosh, oh golly, oh gee,
  Nothing ever happens to me.
  Nothing exciting, no, not to me—
  Not like Gobo or Red or Mokey,
  Gosh, oh golly, oh gee,
  Nothing ever happens to me."

Mokey stopped and sat down next to Wembley. "What's the matter, Wembley?" she asked. "Aren't you feeling well?"

"No," Wembley sighed. "Something exciting has happened to every-one today but me. I just saw Boober, and even *he* seems pretty happy. He had a pile of really dirty-looking socks to wash. He said it was one of the most exciting loads of laundry he's ever seen."

"Yes," Mokey agreed. "That would be exciting for Boober."

"I saw Red, too," Wembley sighed, "and she's finally figured out how to do a triple-scoop somersault. She's very excited about it."

"Yes," said Mokey. "She would be excited about that."

"And Gobo finally discovered the path to the Twisting, Turning Tun-nel, and he's so excited about it that he set off this morning before I even woke up. You know, Mokey," Wembley sighed again, "nothing exciting ever happens to me."

"Well," said Mokey, "you're going to do something exciting right now."

"I am?" said Wembley.

"Yes," Mokey answered. "You're coming with me to pick radishes."

"Oh," said Wembley. It wasn't quite what he had in mind. But Wem-bley, who was a very agreeable Fraggle, agreed to help, and so off they went to the Garden.

Anyway, that's why both Mokey and Wembley were waiting for Junior to stop raking, and finally he did. He stretched, and, yawning a great, gaping yawn, walked to the far side of the Garden to take a nap under a tree.

Now was Mokey and Wembley's chance. They slipped out of their hiding place and into the Garden.

"I'll take the right row and you take the left," Mokey said to Wembley.

"Right," said Wembley.

"No, left," Mokey answered.

"Right," said Wembley, "I'll take the left."

"Right," said Mokey.

It was the kind of conversation that can make you dizzy, and can't go on for long.

"Okay," said Mokey. "I'll stay here and you go over there."

"Got you!" Wembley agreed, and they both set to work.

According to ancient Fraggle custom, Wembley whispered the radish wish before he started picking:

"Radish red, radish bright,
  Pick a radish in moonlight.
  Pick a radish in the sun
  Pick a radish just for fun.

"Then wish upon a radish bright
  And your wish will soon take flight.
  I wish I may, I wish I might
  Have my radish wish—all right?"

Wembley shut his eyes and wished that something exciting would happen to him. And suddenly it did.

CHAPTER TWO

"Mokey," Wembley whispered through the row of radish leaves, "you've got to see this!"

"In a minute," said Mokey. She was in the middle of thinking how interesting it was that *wiggly worms* rhymed with *giggly germs*.

"But you've *got* to see this," Wembley insisted. "It's the biggest radish I've ever seen. It may be the biggest radish in the whole world! I'll bet it's as big as twenty-three regular-sized radishes!"

"Oh, all right," Mokey said, easing through a row of radishes. And then she stopped short, her mouth open.

"You're right!" she gasped. "I've never seen anything like it! This radish would feed eighteen Fraggles for eighteen days!"

"Isn't it exciting!" said Wembley, jumping up and down. "Just wait until Gobo and Red and Boober see *this*!"

"But I don't know how we're going to pick this radish by ourselves!" Mokey said.

"I know," said Wembley. "We'll pull very, very hard."

Together Mokey and Wembley tugged at the huge leafy stem, but the giant radish wouldn't budge.

"Now what?" said Wembley.

"Why don't you push on the other side, and I'll keep pulling," Mokey suggested.

"Good idea!" Wembley cried, and ran around to the other side of the radish.

And so they began, shouting all kinds of encouraging things like "PUSH AND PULL! HEAVE AND HO!" At first, the giant radish still refused to move. Then slowly, very slowly, it began to inch its way out of the soil.

"It's coming!" Wembley cried. "Pull a little harder!"

Mokey pulled as hard as she could. Wembley pushed as hard as he could. Suddenly the earth crumbled, and the radish pulled free.

But there was one thing they had not thought of, and that was what would happen next. What happened was this: As the earth moved and crumbled under his feet, it created a landslide, and Wembley slipped, slid, yelped, and fell

> down,
> > down,
> > > down,

into the giant hole that the giant radish had left in the Garden. As he fell, the earth fell in after him and covered him right up.

CHAPTER THREE

SIRENS wailed. Red warning lights flashed off and on, and emergency patrol units rushed to the rescue. Doozers were running in all directions.

"There's been a cave-in at the refining plant!" one Doozer shouted. "Hurry! We need all the help we can get!"

In order to understand what happened next, you will need to know a few things about Doozers.

First of all, Doozers are about six inches tall, which makes them knee-high to a Fraggle. Doozers live in Fraggle Rock, too, far below the Fraggles' caves.

Unlike Fraggles, Doozers work all the time. They work because they love to work, and the work they love most is building. Their constructions are spread throughout the caves and tunnels of Fraggle Rock.

Luckily, Fraggles find Doozer constructions delicious. Doozer buildings are made from Doozer sticks, which Fraggles love to eat. Doozers are very pleased that Fraggles eat their buildings, because if Fraggles did not eat their buildings, Doozers would quickly run out of room to build.

And why do Fraggles love Doozer sticks? They love them because they love radishes, and most Doozer sticks are made from radishes—only the Fraggles don't know it. The Fraggles also don't know that the radish refining plant is directly under Junior Gorg's Garden. Every day, hundreds of Doozers busily drill holes through Junior's radishes. Then they grind the radish bits into radish dust and mold the dust into Doozer sticks.

So you see, a serious cave-in at the refining plant would be a disaster. Without the refining plant, Doozers would not be able to make Doozer sticks. Without Doozer sticks, there would be no Doozer constructions. And without Doozer constructions, there would be no Doozer sticks for Fraggles to eat.

But the Doozers were not worried about Doozer sticks or building right now. Right now they had a big problem on their hands, and that big problem happened to be Wembley Fraggle. When the first rescue team arrived, they realized that it was not really a cave-in at all, but a Fraggle who had fallen through and landed right in the middle of their refining plant.

It was rather like having a moose fall through the roof of your house into your bedroom. What would you do? You couldn't push him back up through the roof, and a moose is too big to fit through the door and out of your room. The Doozers now faced a similar problem, one that was about to challenge the best Doozer minds.

CHAPTER FOUR

WHEN Mokey realized that Wembley had disappeared down the radish hole, she knew she had to do something, and she had to do it fast. She ran as quickly as she could to the Great Hall, which is in the center of Fraggle Rock, and sounded the alarm. It echoed through the caverns and tunnels, and soon every Fraggle was on the way.

They gathered around Mokey and she told them the story of Wembley and how he had been buried in the radish hole. Fraggles gasped. Fraggles gulped. Fraggles shuddered. And soon hundreds of Fraggles were headed out to the Gorgs' Garden to rescue Wembley.

Wembley, in the meantime, had taken a good bonk on the head on his way down the radish hole, so he was out cold when he crashed into the Doozers' refining plant.

While he lay there, Doozer architects, planners, and designers were already hard at work. Wembley was being measured, mapped, and surveyed. Blueprints were being drawn while the chief Bulldoozers huddled in conference. All Doozer stick production had ceased. Operation Fraggle was under way.

"There's no telling what that foolish Fraggle will do when he wakes up," Bolt Doozer said. "He'll probably start singing or dancing in that silly way of theirs." The others shuddered at the thought, and a wave of nervous whispers rippled through the group.

"Maybe we should put him in a cage," Flange Doozer suggested, "or tie him up, so he can't move."

Slowly Wembley was coming to. He had no idea where he was or how he had gotten there. To tell the truth, he wasn't too eager to find out, especially since the first words he thought he heard were *cage* and *tie him up.*

Wembley lay there quietly and kept his eyes closed, hoping he was just having a strange dream.

"Maybe we should keep him here," another Doozer suggested. "He could be our official Doozer stick taster."

Doozer sticks? Wembley thought, realizing he was hungry. He opened his eyes and raised his head.

"Don't move, don't dance, and whatever you do, don't sing," a Doozer voice boomed through a megaphone. "We've got you surrounded!"

Wembley froze. "Of course," he said. "I mean, of course not—I won't. I wouldn't! I hardly ever dance or sing, and certainly not right after I wake up! I'll sit very, very quietly," Wembley promised. "You won't even know I'm here."

"Humph," Bolt grunted, "I doubt that."

"Ummm, by the way," Wembley said, "where is here?"

"Our refining plant," Bolt answered. "And believe me, you weren't invited!"

Wembley looked around as best he could. He had no idea what a refining plant was. He could see some machines, a pile of Doozer sticks, and a large mound of something that looked like salt. Hundreds of Doozers were hard at work with cranes and shovels, enlarging a tunnel.

Wingnut Doozer approached Wembley with something that looked like a long piece of string. *Oh, no!* gulped Wembley. *They* have *decided to tie me up.* "Please don't!" he cried. "You can see I can't move very far" (which was true; he couldn't). "And I promised I wouldn't" (which was true; he had). But all Wingnut did was measure his leg and then write something down in her notebook.

She turned to Bolt and showed him her calculations. "If we could temporarily remove either his legs or his head, we could get him through the southeast tunnel."

Wembley gulped. "I hate to mention this," he said nervously, "but I'm kind of attached to my legs *and* my head."

"Look, Fraggle," Bolt said, not unkindly, "we're just trying to get you out of here, and we're working on every possible angle."

Just then, a group of Doozer schoolchildren, led by their teacher, filed
into the refining plant. All Doozer children must attend F.A.S. (Fraggle
Avoidance School) before they are allowed to work on the construction
crews in Fraggle Rock. They learn dodging techniques, sidestepping strat-
egies, and all the fine arts of avoiding a Fraggle. When the Doozer
teacher heard there was a Fraggle in the refining plant, he decided to let
the class have a look.

"Wow," one of them cried, "he's a giant!"

"No, I'm not," Wembley said. "Gorgs are giants!" But then Wembley
looked at the tiny Doozer child, who was about three inches tall. "I sup-
pose to you, I *do* look like a giant," Wembley said rather sadly.

The teacher had a long, pointed stick. Wembley was getting nervous
again. *What are they going to do now?* he worried. *I hope they're not going to
poke holes in me with that stick!* The teacher pointed the stick at one of

Wembley's feet. "Note the large, odd-shaped foot area," the teacher said to the class.

The stick began to tickle. Wembley giggled. The children huddled together. "Don't be afraid," the teacher reassured them. "You will often hear Fraggles making that noise."

"I was just laughing," Wembley tried to explain.

"You must watch out for Fraggle feet while on a construction crew," the teacher went on, ignoring Wembley's remark. "Fraggle feet can be very dangerous while jumping, dancing, hopping, or skipping, and you could possibly get thumped."

"I would never thump you," Wembley said. "Gorgs do that, not Fraggles!"

The teacher still ignored Wembley. "While we are here, class,

I would like you to note the fine quality of this radish dust," and he pointed the stick toward the mound near Wembley.

"Oh," said Wembley, "that's what it is! I thought it smelled familiar."

Wembley turned and sniffed the radish dust. He felt a tickle in his throat. He felt a tickle in his nose. Wembley sniffled; Wembley snuffled; Wembley tried to stop it, but he couldn't. He let out a sneeze that had the force of a hurricane, and Doozers were blown in all directions.

Some kinds of sneezes can't help but come in pairs, and this was certainly that kind of sneeze. Wembley sneezed a second enormous *ker-chooooo!*, and part of the ceiling gave way, showering soil and raining pebbles on top of the Doozers.

CHAPTER FIVE

"OH, no!" Wembley cried. "I'm sorry! I didn't mean to sneeze...."

No one answered him. No one even heard him. Doozers were running for their shovels and cranes to begin the rescue operation.

"Let me help," Wembley said as he began scooping away handfuls of dirt.

"Stop!" Bolt cried. Wembley stopped.

"Please *don't* help," Bolt said grimly. "Fraggle help spells Doozer disaster! Just stay put and don't breathe."

"Sure, you bet," Wembley said. "I'm sorry. I don't know how it happened. I don't even know how I got here!"

"Well, I know how you're going to leave," Bolt grumbled under his breath.

Soon every Doozer was safe and accounted for. But there was no time to rest. They had to get back to Operation Fraggle.

At last all systems were go. "Okay, Fraggle," Bolt said, "roll over to your left!"

"Right," Wembley said. He rolled over, as carefully as he could, onto his stomach. He found himself on a long flatcar.

"Now, Fraggle," Bolt said, "don't do a thing."

The flatcar began to move, and Wembley bumped along, wondering all the while where he was going.

It had been a lot of work for the Doozers to enlarge the tunnel that led to the Fraggles' Great Hall. And they would have to work quickly after they dropped Wembley off to fill it in again. They certainly did not want any more Fraggles showing up in their refining plant!

At last Wembley felt the flatcar bump to a stop.

"This is it," Bolt said. "Good-bye, Fraggle." And he and the other Doozers quickly disappeared down the tunnel.

Wembley sat up and looked around. "I'm home!" he cried when he realized he was in the Great Hall. But something was wrong—he couldn't see any Fraggles anywhere!

CHAPTER SIX

WEMBLEY looked all over the Great Hall without seeing one Fraggle. "Where *is* everyone?" he wondered. He ran up and down tunnels and looked in every cave. "Finally I have an exciting story to tell, and there's no one here to tell it to!" he grumbled. "Oh, rocks and ruts!"

At last he found himself at the entrance to the Gorgs' Garden. He stopped short. And suddenly he remembered what had happened! He remembered the giant radish and the big hole and everything!

"Maybe Mokey is still in the Garden!" he cried. "I can tell her about my adventure!" And he climbed outside to find her.

The first Fraggle Wembley saw was Boober. His back was to Wembley. Wembley tapped him on the shoulder. Boober turned around. "A ghost!" Boober cried, and fainted.

Every Fraggle turned and looked in Wembley's direction.

"Wembley's back!" Gobo cried. "It's a miracle!"

Boober raised his head. "He's back from the dead!" he gasped, and fainted again.

Wembley didn't know what they were talking about. "What's going on?" he asked.

"You fell down the radish hole," Mokey said. "Don't you remember?"

"Yeah," Red chimed in. "Where did you come from? We've been digging for *hours*!" And she pointed to a big ditch. Fraggles were standing around it with picks and shovels, looking exhausted.

"Wow!" said Wembley. "Did you do that all for me? I've been where the Doozers live! Gosh, I've got so many exciting things to tell you. Doozers think that we're giants! Can you believe it? They're afraid we'll thump them. And..."

"*Sure*, Wembley," Mokey said as she patted him on the back. She glanced at Gobo. "I think you'd better lie down, Wembley. You seem to have a nasty bump on your head."

"But it was all so interesting!" Wembley said. "The Doozers make radish dust. I don't know why, but they do. I was afraid they were going to grind me up into dust, too."

"Right, Wembley," Red said, not believing a word.

Wembley gave up trying to explain. "Gee, I'm glad to be back," he said. "I've had enough excitement to last a long time."

"We're glad you are, too," the puzzled Fraggles said as they headed back to Fraggle Rock, carrying Boober and the giant radish.

"Now you go take a nap," Mokey said to Wembley. "And we'll fix a welcome-home radish feast. When you wake up, maybe you'll remember what *really* happened."

Wembley nodded. He knew that no one believed him. Still, for a long time (maybe even a week and a half), he watched the Doozers working in Fraggle Rock. But they never said a word, and they never seemed to recognize him. Eventually even Wembley decided that it must have been a dream after all.

But to this day, Wembley is still very careful about where he walks when there are Doozers around, and he is also very careful about wishing that something exciting would happen to him.